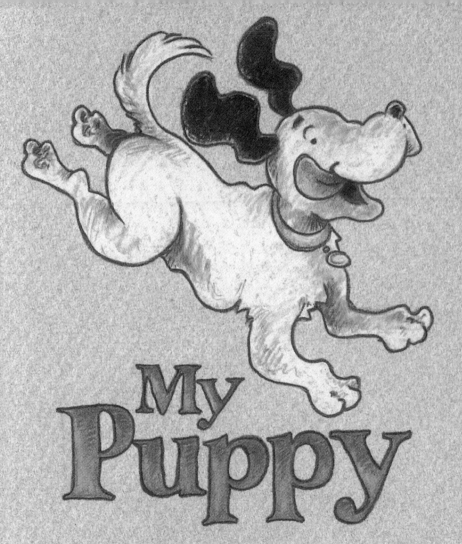

My Puppy

Written by Inez Greene Illustrated by Larry Nolte

📖 GoodYearBooks

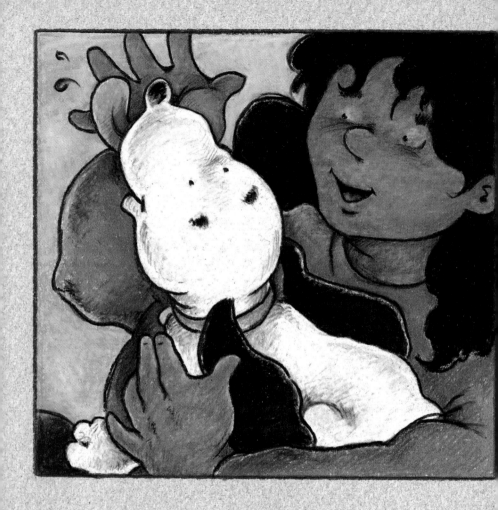

My puppy licks my fingers.

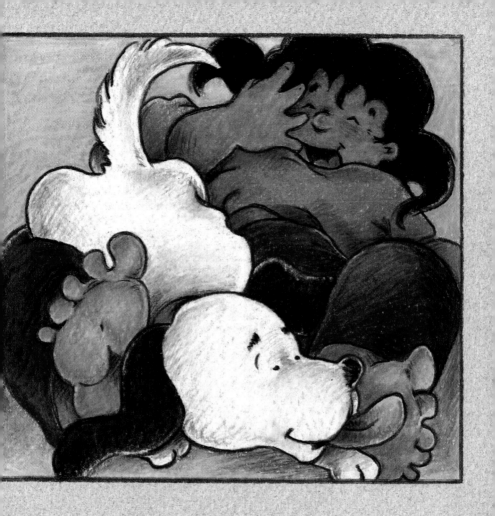

He licks my toes.

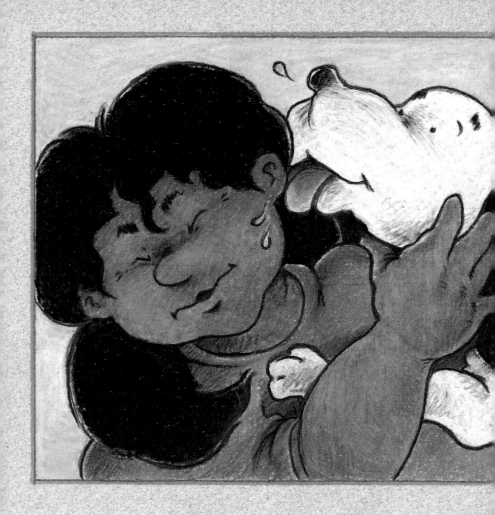

He licks my ear.

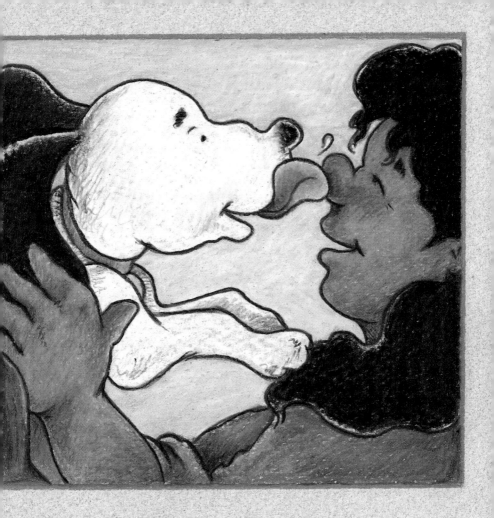

He licks my nose.

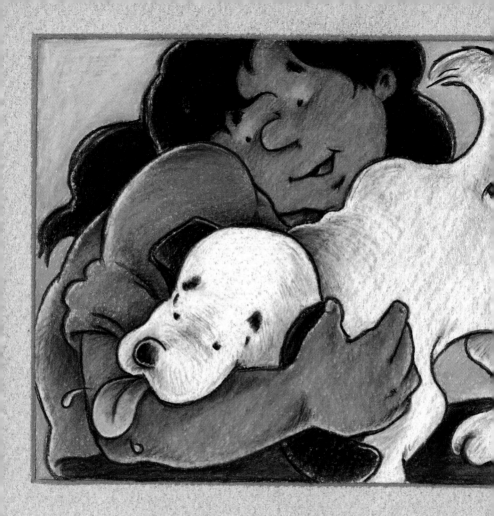

He licks my elbow.

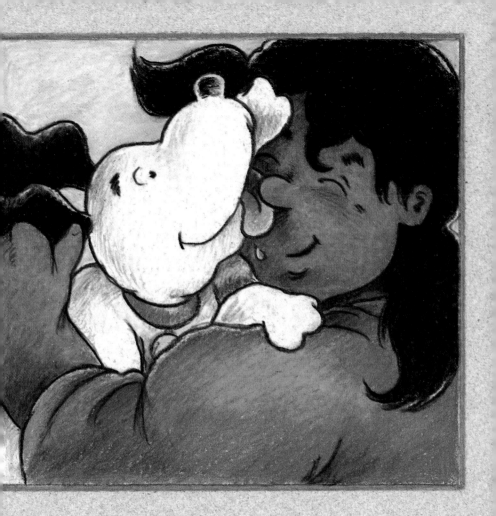

He licks my face.

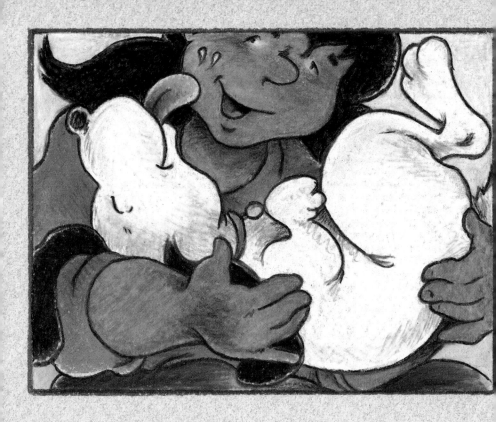

My puppy licks me
all over the place!